GHOS

Anne Greig

Illustrated by
Maureen Bradley

Chapter I

The day Sam dreaded had finally arrived. They were moving house. From his window he could see the high, blue furniture van belonging to the removal firm. He looked round his bare room. His mattress stood against the wall. The small legs had been unscrewed from his bed, tied together with string, and were lying next to the mattress. Without curtains the room seemed unnaturally bright, showing up the dirty marks on the wallpaper like his finger marks on his art paper when he tried to use charcoal. There was a line of dirt where his table had been against the wall. The remains of a dusty cobweb hung down unsupported.

Angrily Sam squashed his poor bear into the bulging carrier bag, along with two Lego pieces and a handful of marbles. In a corner were some stickers that had fallen down behind the cupboard, unnoticed until the furniture had been removed.

From the very first visit to the new house he had told them he wasn't moving, but his parents had taken no notice of him. His mother had waded through the nettles and briars, saying how wonderful the garden could be. His father had peered at the roof and guttering, saying he could soon fix the water that was pouring in a waterfall over the front door. The inside was even worse. As soon as he stepped through the door, Sam's nose detected the most vile smell he had ever encountered. It was partly due to the damp that showed in grey and black patches all the way up the walls. But it was not just that. Sam sniffed cautiously in disbelief. It was the smell of cats who had been shut up in the house all day.

As he wandered deeper into the house along a maze of passages, away from the open door, the smell became stronger. He went up the stairs and opened a door that led off a halfway landing. It led into a small room with a high ceiling, the only light coming from a small window which was low down in one corner. Sam felt himself choking, the air was so foul.

"Blimey! Things must have been bad for the old girl near the end," said his dad, pushing past him to open the window.

"What do you mean?" asked Sam.

"Well, the old lady who owned the house was eighty," explained Dad. "The house was much too big for her. As she became ill I imagine she couldn't be bothered with the upstairs. Although it's obvious the cats did!" he added as an afterthought.

"Mum, this is awful! We can't live here," declared Sam to his mother as she entered the room. She was smiling to herself and wore that dreamy expression that Sam recognised immediately. Oh no! She was making plans.

"This can be the bathroom," she announced as if he had not spoken.

"Well, I'm not moving in here. You'll have to leave me behind," Sam cried and he stamped out of the room.

Along the landing were two large bedrooms, each hanging with cobwebs and thick with dust. Sam looked across the wilderness of a garden to the field beyond. His heart sank. He knew that this was just what his parents had been searching for, an old house with a large garden and some land. They enjoyed restoring old things, doing alterations and decorating. But what about me, thought Sam. He remembered his comfortable room, arranged just as he wanted it—a corner for Lego, his bookshelves and his bed tucked under the sloping roof. He glanced round the dreary room he was in, absentmindedly picking at the rotten wood of the window frame. It would mean leaving his friends, too. He would miss Chris and James. What about school? Would he have to go to another school? His stomach lurched at the thought. He bit his lip as tears stung his eyes.

The bedroom door creaked and the old metal latch clicked. A shadow on the wall slowly moved as the door squeaked open.

"Boo!" In jumped Rob, his elder brother,
grinning at his own joke.

"Get lost, Rob," said Sam crossly, taking his
anger out on his brother.

"Come on, kiddo, it's great! I've been round
the back. There are steps leading to a balcony

and a huge barn! And at the other side is a workshop with a loft above it. I'm going to ask Dad if we can have that for ourselves. We could fit it out, get a snooker table."

Rob was just as bad as Mum and Dad. Who would want to live in a dump like this?

"I've told them I'm not living here," Sam shouted and stormed off back to the car.

That had been two months ago. His feelings had not changed. It had been arranged that he could still go to his old school, travelling by car each day, so his worst fear had been avoided. His parents had tried to explain all the advantages to him; more space to play, a field with a slope for sledging in winter, trees to climb, the loft to share with Rob as a private den. There was even some cautious talk about a dog. He had argued with them, but they would not change their minds. Even when they heard the house was haunted, they were not put off. Now he had to face the fact that tonight he would have a new home.

Chapter II

By evening, the family and all their possessions were at "Moss Bank", the new house. It was not quite accurate to say that they had moved in. Most of the furniture and carpets had been carefully stored in the large barn. The family had spent the afternoon dragging out the old smelly carpets and lino from all the rooms. These were now piled in a heap in the field. Each room had been thoroughly swept and aired to make it a bit fresher. They installed just enough furniture to manage—their beds, a sofa, a table and four chairs. There was so much work to be done that it was a waste of time unpacking things only to move them from room to room as work progressed.

After a tea of sausages and beans cooked on a camping stove, Sam sat at the table with his parents. They were all tired, but Mum was still planning what she would do.

"We can knock down this wall between the kitchen and the bathroom to make the kitchen larger. Then we'll move the bathroom upstairs to the cats' room," (as they now called the smelly little room), "and that way we'll have a lovely, big kitchen and the bathroom will be nearer to the bedrooms," she explained, pleased with her ideas.

"Hang on," said Dad. "If we move the bathroom to the opposite end of the house, it means I will have to put in a completely new set of drains."

"You are so clever," said Mum flattering him, "you can do it." She was very cunning when she wanted her own way.

"How long is all this going to take?" asked Sam, regretting the loss of his comfortable old home.

"Oh, don't worry, Dad will soon do it. And you can help," she added cheerfully.

Sam was not so enthusiastic about that. "I'm not a plumber," he grumbled.

"No love, but you can work in the garden— chop down overgrown trees and do all sorts of jobs. The sort of jobs you get paid for . . ." she added coaxingly.

That sounds better, thought Sam.

Suddenly they were sitting in the dark. "Oh no, the lights have fused!" complained Dad. "Where did you pack the torch? Have we got candles?"

"We have them, but which box they are in I really don't know. What about the torch you keep in the car?" Mum reminded him.

"Good thinking," answered Dad. In the dim light from the window Sam saw his father rise to his feet but suddenly freeze, as if taken aback. Sam turned towards a sound at the doorway and gasped in fright. He felt the hairs on his scalp tingle. There, silhouetted against the faint light of the hallway, was a large grey shape, moving stealthily towards them. Sam heard the sharp intake of breath behind him as his mother saw the shape looming closer. She grabbed Sam's shoulder and drew him back close to her. Sam sensed her fear, and there was no reassurance in her touch. This must be the ghost they had scoffed about, he thought, as his heartbeat thudded loudly in his ears.

The ghost raised its arms and reached out towards them uttering a low moaning sound that chilled Sam's blood.

"Whoo whoo!" came a hoarse voice, followed by, "Ow drat!" as the ghost stumbled, tripping over his sheet. He collapsed in a tangled heap, arms groping to find a way out.

"What the dickens . . . ?" said Dad. "Oh, it's you, Rob. You idiot! You really had me there," and he began to chuckle.

"You great fool," said Mum crossly. "Poor Sam was scared to bits."

"You were scared too," chipped in Sam. "I could feel you shaking."

"Well, just a bit," she conceded and started to laugh as Rob struggled to disentangle himself from his ghost costume. The next moment they were all laughing together, partly with relief and partly because they had been so easily fooled.

"Well," said Dad at last, "I'd better go and mend the fuse."

"No need, Dad," said Rob. "I switched off the electricity at the mains. I'll go and put it back on now."

"You'll have to do better than that to scare us away," chuckled Mum.

"Whose ghost is supposed to haunt the house anyway?" asked Sam anxiously.

"Well, no one has said exactly," mused Dad. "They just said the house was haunted." At this point Rob came back and joined the conversation, answering Sam's question.

"The woman in white with her head under her arm," he announced gleefully, prancing about, "searching for a place to rest in her old house. She wanders round and round the house, totally confused because Mum has changed all the rooms about!"

Mum gave him a playful push saying, "Get along with you, you great fool."

Sam had been amused by Rob's performance but it aroused the doubts he had at the back of his mind. Who had told them that the house was haunted? Were there really such things as ghosts? Would they be as grey and sinister as Rob had appeared?

"Do you believe in ghosts, Mum?" he asked.

Mum glanced at him and knew he wanted a serious answer. "Well love, I don't really know. I've never seen anything ghostly to make me believe. But there again, there have been so

many people who have claimed to have seen ghosts that I would not ignore the possibility. But don't worry about it," she added, giving him a quick cuddle. "It was probably someone starting a false rumour to put us off buying this place."

"Enough of this spooky talk," interrupted Dad. "What would you say to lighting a bonfire of all those stinking carpets?"

"Oh yes," cried Sam jumping up. "Can I invite Chris and James round?"

"Well, not really, Sam," replied Dad. "It would take me half an hour in the car to go and get them and then I'd have to take them all the way back. We can have a house-warming party with just the family. Have we any lemonade?"

"No, but there are a few cans of coke and I can make beefburgers for afterwards," suggested Mum.

"O.K." said Sam, disappointed. A bonfire would be good fun, but it would have been better with a few friends to share it.

Chapter III

Over the next few weeks there was plenty to do.
Rob and Sam set to work in their loft. The
workshop building had been built into the
hillside. From the front you could walk into the
workshop and up the stairs into the loft above.
In the far corner at the back of the loft was a
door. If you went through this, you walked on
to the slope of the hill at the back. In this part
of the country it was common to see old houses
and farm buildings like this, tucked snugly
against the hill so that they were surrounded on
three sides by soil. They were built like this for
warmth and to reduce the draughts in an area
where the weather could turn very cold and
windy in any season of the year.

Sam liked having the two entrances on different levels. He called the far door his escape door. If any unwelcome visitor came up the workshop stairs he could escape through the back into the trees and bushes behind. The last occupants of the loft had been hens. Sam and Rob had to move nesting boxes from the walls and take out food troughs. They needed a wheelbarrow and shovels to clean up the floor.

When it was clean and scrubbed, they painted the walls white and began to move in some of their things. Mum said they could have two old armchairs and the old kitchen table. Rob set it up near the window to do his modelling work.

During the packing up at the old house, Sam had found a box of old plastic soldiers and army vehicles that had once belonged to Rob. He was busy arranging his new-found toys in a corner one afternoon when he heard a car. Looking down, he saw Grandad struggling to get something very large out of the car.

"Hey, give me a hand, you chaps!" he called up to them.

"What's he got now?" wondered Rob, peering out of the window. "Oh, great! It's the train set." He dashed down the stairs to help lift out a large board with a train layout fixed to it.

"Here you are, boys. I promised you could have this when you had enough room for it."

"It's great, Grandad. Thanks," said Rob delighted. "Will you show us how to set it up?"

"I'm sure I could," replied Grandad eagerly, pleased to be asked to play.

Setting up the train occupied Rob and Grandad for the next hour or so. Sam was in the way, so he decided to go and make an aerial rope way for his soldiers on the trees at the top of the garden. He tied a string to the highest branch of the apple tree and secured it at ground level near the gate. He climbed the tree, fixed the pulley at the top and tried it out with one of the soldiers. He watched him glide smoothly to the ground. Perfect! From his perch he could see most of the garden. Mum was right. The garden must have been lovely years ago before it became neglected. It could be made attractive again with a lot of work. Even now, in its overgrown state, the leaves of all the different trees and bushes were showing beautiful colours.

The whole garden was on a steep slope. The house was at the bottom of the slope. It had once been a small farm and attached to the house were the farm buildings. Next to the kitchen was a stable and a byre for the cattle.

These, like the workshop, were built into the hillside to keep the animals snug and warm in the long winter months. Because of this style of building, it was possible to walk out of the end door of the barn on to the slope of the hill, just like you could from the loft above the workshop.

The area at the top had once been an orchard with apple and plum trees. These had now been joined by thorn bushes and elder trees which made it seem more like a jungle. It was a good place to play. From here, Sam could look down over the whole area. To the right there was a flight of steps going down to the yard between the workshop and the barn. To the left of the barn there were more steps going down through the garden.

The garden itself was like a giant staircase, made of terraces. At the top was the orchard. Then there was a steep bank down to the next level which was a shrubbery. At the edge of the shrubbery was a wall dropping down to the lower level where there was a lawn and flower garden. After this, there was another wall going down to the path with the vegetable garden beyond. That was how it was meant to be, but at present, it was so overgrown that it was difficult to see all these features.

As Sam glanced down, he saw a boy walk along the bottom path and disappear round the end of the house. He frowned. Who's that, he wondered?

He went down the steps to see who it was, but the unknown visitor was no longer around.

"Did you bring a boy with you?" he asked his Grandma when he went into the house.

"No, Sam. Just Grandad. He's a great boy," chuckled Grandma. "I bet he's playing with the train set."

"I've just seen a boy in the garden," persisted Sam.

"Perhaps it's one of the neighbours that we haven't met yet," suggested his mother. "Is he still there?"

"No, he's gone," said Sam, disappointed because as yet he had not found any children near enough to play with.

"Don't worry, he'll be back," Mum reassured him. "He was probably just seeing what we are like." She turned back to Grandma and continued her conversation about wallpaper. Sam felt that they were not really interested and he returned to the garden feeling lonely and puzzled.

Chapter IV

During the next few weeks, the family continued tidying up the house and buildings, getting ready for the real alterations to begin. At last the letter came, saying that the planning department at the Civic Centre approved of the plans, and work could start.

"The first thing we do is to put in the new bathroom in the cats' room," declared Dad. "Once that is finished, we can take out the old one from downstairs and extend the kitchen into the extra space."

"And then we'll have a dream kitchen, just like the adverts!" said Mum, doing a little dance.

"The dream kitchen is still a long way off!" remarked Dad. "Remember, I have to dig all the new drains round the house first."

"We will all help," she soothed him.

"Mum, can Chris come this Saturday?" asked Sam.

"Not this weekend, love. We have to go to town early to buy the equipment and building materials. We'll be hard at work all weekend. I won't have time to run backwards and forwards with children."

"Oh, Mum, I told him we could make a den," moaned Sam.

"Well, you'll just have to tell him that you'll make it some other time," she answered sharply.

"It's not fair. I hardly ever see him now. You said that I'd soon make new friends but there is no one round here to play with," continued Sam resentfully.

"We'll see about next weekend," promised his mother, putting him off.

Next weekend would be the same, thought Sam as he wandered up to the orchard. All their promises about it being a marvellous place to play were worthless if you had no one to share it with. He went to inspect the aerial rope way, but it had become soggy and tangled with leaves. The garden looked much bigger now than when they first came. He and Rob had helped Mum and Dad cut down the thorn bushes and briars that had invaded the orchard. They had pulled out the nettles and some of the larger weeds from lower down the garden, so it looked less like a wilderness. Now the golden leaves of the maple tree were beginning to fall, so it was possible to see down the whole length of the pathway.

Sam's eye was caught by a movement at the very bottom of the vegetable patch. He stared. The boy was there again. He seemed to be peering into the garden shed in the corner. What a cheek, thought Sam. He set off down the path to ask him who he thought he was, poking his nose in other people's property. Sam was almost at the bottom of the steps when the boy turned and looked straight at him, his brown eyes unsmiling. Sam halted. The boy came forward, stepped onto the path and walked up to the wall below the flower garden. He ran his hand along the wall and glanced again at Sam. Then he turned and walked round the end of the house, out of sight.

All this time Sam neither moved or spoke. He appeared to be very still. But inside his head his thoughts were racing. The boy's clothes, he thought, what was it about his clothes that was so odd? He had been wearing a shirt fastened up tight at the neck but no tie, just a scarf. His jacket looked heavy and shapeless. His trousers had looked odd, too, and he had been wearing boots. All this was odd, yet familiar at the same time. And then he remembered. The boy looked like a character out of a book at school. That was it! Sam had been reading about schools in Victorian times and there had been pictures of children dressed just the same as the strange boy; the same clothes, the same forlorn look. But why should a boy dressed like this appear in Sam's garden? There were no other boys in the neighbouring houses who could have dressed up to play a trick or for fancy dress. What could the explanation be then?

Suddenly Sam's thoughts stopped racing and became very still as one possibility came to his mind. He felt certain he was right, unlikely as it seemed. The ghost of Moss Bank was not a woman in white as Rob had jokingly portrayed. It was a boy, as real-looking as anyone in the street, given away only by the fact that his clothes were out of time. And yet, Sam had not been afraid. There was nothing to be afraid of. He was just a boy, a sad boy, but not frightening. Sam curiously retraced the steps of the boy, but the garden looked the same as usual. What had the boy been looking at, he wondered.

When eventually Sam returned to the house, his parents were deep in conversation. Sam felt again his disappointment over his plans for the weekend. Why should he tell them about his mystery boy? They would just think he was trying to pull a stunt like Rob's. No, he thought, if the boy wanted them to see him he would show himself when he was ready. Hugging his secret close he went to bed.

Chapter V

The next day as they ate lunch, another meal out of tins cooked on a camp stove, Sam questioned his parents about the history of the house. "Who built this house?" he asked.

"I'm not sure. It might be in the house deeds if we had a look," suggested Dad.

"What are deeds?" Sam enquired.

"Papers and documents saying who has owned it at different times," replied Dad.

"When do you think it stopped being used as a farm?" asked Sam.

"Quite a long time since I'd say, perhaps fifty years ago even."

"Would the deeds tell us all about the people?" persisted Sam.

"No, just about the owners. Why are you so curious?" asked Dad.

"Oh, I just wondered," Sam muttered.

"If you are really interested, you could go to the records office at the city archives. They keep all sorts of papers there—parish records, census returns, newspapers—all sorts of things," explained Dad. "You would certainly find out what you wanted to know. Is it for school or something?"

"No," said Sam again, "I just wondered."

"Well, if you really want to find out, I'll take you myself and help you, but it will have to wait until I have more time."

"Thanks, Dad," replied Sam, glad to know that he could find out, but disappointed that he would have to wait.

This must have shown on his face because his father said, "You could make that time come quicker if you help. How would you like to give me a hand to mark out the new drains?"

Sam agreed, and went to change into his old jeans. He spent the afternoon with his dad, measuring and marking out the lines that the drains would take.

"We have to go from this corner, along the path and then straight to the septic tank," said Dad.

"What's that?" asked Sam.

"It's a large tank to collect all the waste water from the house. In the town, the drains go into the main sewer, but in the country each house has its own mini-system called a septic tank. There are tiny living things called bacteria in the waste that work naturally to make the water clean again, and the clean water is released into the field drains, eventually going back to the river." Dad pointed, indicating the area beyond the fence. "Our tank is over there."

"I've seen that manhole cover, but I didn't know what it was for," replied Sam.

"Well, that's where our drains are heading for."

"But if we take a straight line, it means knocking down that garden wall," pointed out Sam. "The wall is holding up all the soil from the garden above. What if there's a landslide?"

"I don't think there is any danger of that," replied Dad. "That soil has been there for a hundred years and will be very solid by now. I know it's a nuisance having to cut across the hillside, but if we went round, it would take a lot longer. We can get a JCB to do the work beyond the wall, but on this side it will have to be done by hand. Whoever built that wall originally made a good job of it. We will be able to build it up again once the drains are finished."

By evening the garden was crossed by white tapes held in place by wooden pegs.

"We can start digging first thing tomorrow," declared Dad. "I'm ready for a cup of tea," he added, heading for the kitchen.

Sam decided to have a game with his soldiers and went up the steps to the orchard where he had left them. He collected them from their ambush positions in the trees and bushes, and went to the loft to get the vehicles. As he came down the terraces, he thought that the tapes looked like a network of roads marked out. The broken-up soil in the vegetable patch was like a disaster area. Sam immediately saw the possibilities for a game. This could be the road to a town where there had been an earthquake, he thought. He set his vehicles out in a convoy, bringing supplies to the stricken area. He placed his plastic men near a pile of stones as if they were searching for survivors. He drove his Red Cross ambulance over rough soil to move the injured.

Sam did not know how long the ghost boy had been watching him, but when he turned towards the garden gate, the boy was standing there. They stared at each other. Again Sam felt no fear. The ghost boy seemed just an ordinary boy, apart from his clothes. His hair was brown and rather longer than most boys Sam knew. He looked a little older than Sam, about twelve years old, maybe. He was stockily built and well tanned, as if he spent days out of doors. He glanced at Sam's soldiers. He seemed to find them fascinating.

"I was just setting them up for a game," Sam explained, moving one of the soldiers to a better position. "This will be a trench tomorrow." He indicated the taped area with his hand. He stopped suddenly and wondered what he was doing talking to a ghost. Was the boy a ghost or was he real? Could he hear? Would he answer?

The ghost boy turned and looked along the route of the drains. He walked to the place where the route cut through the high wall against the bank. He stared at it for a few moments and then turned back to Sam with a look of great sadness.

"We'll build it up again," said Sam, as if the boy had protested about the wall.

"First sign of madness, kiddo," grinned Rob as he bounced round the corner of the house. "Talking to yourself! You'd better watch it. They'll come and take you away." He playfully pinned Sam's arms behind his back.

"Ow, get off, Rob," protested Sam.

"The looney bin for you, mate," he continued as Sam squirmed to get free. Rob was O.K. but, at times, having a fourteen-year-old brother was a pain.

"Give over, Rob," said Sam again. He looked towards the ghost boy and caught his eye. He gave Sam a gentle smile and then walked along the path, right in front of Sam and Rob, and round the end of the house as he had the other times.

"Rob!" Sam stopped struggling and turned to look at his brother to see how he had reacted to seeing the boy.

"Do you submit, or must I gif you an injection of zee sleep serum?" said Rob in his mad professor voice. He had not seen the boy. The boy had passed within a metre of Rob's face and he had not seen him. The boy *must* be a ghost!

"You do what you like," said Sam impatiently, not interested in the game in which he was being forced to take part.

"O.K., O.K!" said Rob letting go. "Keep your hair on. Mum sent me to say that it's tea time. You'll never guess what we're having!"

"What?" asked Sam.

"Beans and beefburgers," answered Rob.

"What, again?" grumbled Sam. "The sooner

we get our dream kitchen and a proper cooker the better!"

Sam was quiet that evening as he considered the events of the afternoon. The boy was not visible to Rob, only to Sam. He had communicated with Sam by his looks even if he had not spoken. Why did he haunt the garden? Why was he restless?

"Are you all right, Sam?" inquired his mother. "You're very quiet. Are you tired?"

"I think I'll go to bed," he answered going over to her.

She put her arm round him and gave him a cuddle. "Sorry we've been so busy. I don't seem to have seen you all day."

Sam smiled. "It's O.K. I've been busy, too," he answered. "Mum?"

"Yes?" She looked at him. What would she say if he told her about the ghost boy? No, he decided, she would say he was imagining it or that he was over-tired.

"Nothing. Goodnight."

Chapter VI

The next day Sam rescued his soldiers before Dad buried them in the soil. He set off to go down to the wood. He was not surprised when he was joined by the ghost boy as he went through the narrow garden gate which led to the field. They walked a little way in silence. Sam felt at ease with his silent companion.

"Rob didn't see you," he confided. The boy smiled as if he already knew. "We've not been here long," Sam explained. "The old woman who lived here died." He paused, wondering if talking about death would upset the boy, but it didn't appear to, so Sam continued. "She had let the house get in a terrible mess. It was very neglected. We have all this work to do to put it right. First, we are going to put in a new bathroom and then extend the kitchen." He related all the plans, not realising how like his mother he sounded. It was almost as though he was explaining to himself why he was so much on his own.

They crossed the field and followed the hedge to the edge of the wood. This was one of Sam's favourite places. He sat under a huge oak whose roots spread in all directions like the claws of a giant bird. He took his soldiers out of his pocket and began to set up his game. He became absorbed. The boy crouched down and watched intently.

Sam spoke, half to himself. "Now, you had better go there and defend that hill," he said, placing a man on the curve of a root. The boy reached into his pocket and took something out. He placed it carefully alongside Sam's plastic army. It was a small soldier, made of lead, its paint chipped with use and age. Sam had seen them in museums. He looked up at the

boy delighted, and they exchanged smiles.

For some time Sam played with his strange, silent companion. When he returned home, he felt happier than he had done for weeks. Sam soon got used to finding that he was no longer alone as he played. He would be by the garden shed and the boy would be there. Or he would be in the orchard and the boy would be perched in a tree. Perhaps the ghost boy had been lonely, too, just waiting for a child to live in the house to keep him company. Why did the adults not see him? Sam said nothing to his parents or Rob. What good would it do? No one would believe him anyway and the ghost boy meant no harm.

Each evening Dad progressed a little further with the drains. Soon he had reached the wall below the flower garden. All he had to do was take the wall down, stone by stone, for about two metres. Then the JCB could reach in from the field beyond and dig out the hillside behind the wall, cutting a route through for the drains.

"Phew! Someone made a good job building this wall," said Dad as he struggled to take it apart and put the neat sandstone blocks well out of the way. When he had removed it down to the foundations at the end near the field, he said, "I'll be glad to let the JCB do the rest tomorrow. When they built this wall, somebody must have had the job of filling in all the soil behind the wall by hand, and then levelling the top to make the terrace. Either he liked doing that sort of work or he paid someone to do it for him."

"Would the people who lived here have been rich, Dad?" asked Sam.

"They would have been quite well off. I expect he did pay someone," finished Dad.

The next morning, Sam was sitting in the apple tree at the edge of the orchard when he saw the ghost boy playing among the bushes. As he watched, he saw the boy suddenly appear startled. He was peering intently down the garden towards the kitchen door. Sam followed his gaze and he saw a man emerge from the door, a man dressed in the same style as the ghost boy. He had long side whiskers way past his ears. His boots were dirty, covered with soil. In his hand he held a man's pocket watch and chain, made of gold. It gleamed in the sun as he turned it over in his hands, examining it. Sam blinked because he was confused by what he saw. This man was unknown to Sam and yet the ghost boy seemed to recognise him because he stood up abruptly from his place in the bushes.

It seemed to Sam as though what happened next, he saw in slow motion, as in a dream. The ghost boy, looking angry, ran down the steps in great leaps, and threw himself at the man, snatching at the watch. The man easily held him away with his strong arms. He seemed taken by surprise and tried to move away across the garden. The boy fought and kicked the man, trying all the time to grab the watch.

As they fought and struggled furiously, Sam was filled with a desire to help the boy. He felt as if he was choking, as if he could not breathe. And like in a dream, his body would not move. He was powerless to help.

Sam saw the ghost boy make a final attempt to recover the watch. He saw his foot stumble on the piled-up sandstones. He saw the boy go crashing down, the right side of his head cracking against the stone wall. Sam's head swam as he saw the boy falling. . . .

Chapter VII

"Sam, Sam. Are you all right?" Sam opened his eyes and above him the face of his mother wavered and finally came into focus. She looked shocked and anxious. "Can you hear me? Lie still. You must have fallen from the tree. He's coming round," she said to someone Sam could not see.

Slowly, Sam became aware of his surroundings. Above him, like a network against the blue sky, were the bare branches of the apple tree. He was lying in the damp grass, surrounded by the bitter, earthy smell of decaying leaves. Carefully, he began to move his legs and arms, testing to see if he was hurt. How did he come to be here? As he tried to sit up, he was overcome with dizziness.

"He's moving his limbs. I don't think he's broken anything," he heard his father say. "I'll carry him inside. 'Phone for Doctor MacKay." Sam was carried gently inside only half aware of what was happening.

After he had examined Sam, the doctor advised that Sam should be kept quiet for a couple of days. He appeared to be unharmed if rather dazed. What had caused Sam to faint and fall from the tree was a mystery. Perhaps he was about to go down with some virus, suggested the doctor. Better keep an eye on him.

Indeed, Sam was in a daze, barely aware of what was going on around him, his mind in limbo between past and present. He heard the sound of the tractor approaching and of Dad giving instructions to the man with the JCB about where to start digging. The sound of the engine droned on. His mother persuaded him to drink some hot tea.

"You look as white as a ghost," she said. "Do you feel any better yet?"

"A bit," he replied, and his mind drifted off unhappily to try to recall what he had seen.

"What happened to the boy?" he asked. His mother looked worried and felt his forehead with her hand.

"Just rest," she advised him, concerned that he seemed delirious. She brought her work into the room so that she could keep an eye on him, but she did not talk much. Voices drifted in from the garden.

"Hold it!" Sam heard his father's voice and the sound of the tractor faded as the engine switched off. They must have finished, thought Sam, and he drifted off to sleep.

When he awoke he heard voices talking excitedly but quietly behind him. Obviously his family did not wish to disturb him.

"Are you sure?" asked his mother.

"You should see it, Mum," answered Rob.

"No doubt about it," added Dad. "When we found the first bone I thought it could have been a sheep's skeleton or something. But when we found the skull there was no mistaking it. It's human all right."

"But what do we do? We should tell the police. How old do you think it is?" asked Mum in a worried voice.

Sam heard just this, but he knew with calm certainty what they had found.

"Sam, you're awake!" his mother exclaimed, noticing him, wondering how much he had heard, how much she need tell him. She decided he would have to know sooner or later. She said, "There's been a rather gruesome discovery in the garden." She paused. "They have uncovered a skeleton—a human skeleton. It will mean the police will have to come, probably the Press, too." Sam just stared at her, not seeming to take it in. "He's still dazed," Mum whispered to Dad. "You had better call the police."

"O.K. love," Dad comforted her. "Stay here with the boys ... Rob! Come back here. I don't want you digging about. It is a job for the police. I'll call them now." Rob had been on his way back outside and returned reluctantly, knowing from the tone of his father's voice that this was an order he must obey.

After Dad had 'phoned, they waited together for the police to arrive. Sam said nothing and his parents were quiet. Rob was bursting with excitement and questions.

"Why would they put a body behind a wall? It must have been put there when the wall was built. Do you think it was hidden? It must have been hidden. There must have been some crime. It'll be in all the papers." He wandered to the mirror and posed as he straightened his hair. "I've got it," he exclaimed. "There must have been a murder and that's why this place is supposed to be haunted, except that we've not seen the ghost yet."

Sam turned away, no longer listening to

Rob's wild guesses and theories. Not a murder, just a tragic accident. He relived the scene in his mind's eye and saw again the boy stumble and fall, crashing hard against the stone. He realised that the garden in his mind and the garden today looked similar; only then the wall was being built, whereas today it had been taken down. How easy then to conceal a body, to build up the wall and fill in the soil behind, turning the terrace into an unmarked grave. But why? Why had the unknown man not said there had been an accident? It must have been something to do with the watch. Had he been stealing it? Had he panicked in his guilt? Had no one missed the boy? Who had grieved and worried when he disappeared? How would they ever know? All these questions troubled his mind as they waited.

The police arrived quietly, with no sirens or flashing lights. There was no need to hurry for a body long dead. Photographs were taken. The site was examined by the plainclothes men. Rob and his parents explained to the police how they came to find the skeleton.

At first Sam stayed inside, watching through the window. But after a time he felt drawn by curiosity and sadness to join the group. He stood to the side and stared down into the deep hole. He felt certain that his quiet companion would not appear to him again, now that his body had been discovered. His mother put her arm round his shoulders. He watched as the uniformed policemen arrived with their spades.

"It was an accident," he explained to his mother. She looked at him blankly, so he went on. "He was struggling and he fell. He hit his

head. It was an accident," he repeated.

"What are you talking about?" asked his mother. "What do you mean?"

Sam remembered then that he had never spoken of the ghost boy, and now they would think he was making it up, or talking rubbish because of his fall from the tree. He sighed. "We played armies. He has a lead soldier." His mother stared at him in disbelief. The police inspector had overheard what was said and studied him with interest. "I never knew his name," concluded Sam in a quiet voice. He turned and went back to the house.

The work to uncover the skeleton went on during the late afternoon. The sun, hovering over the hills, cast a warm, golden glow over the autumn garden. Sam's mother came quietly into the sitting room, put on the corner lamp and sat down next to Sam. "They found this," was all she said as she handed him a small, dirty object. Sam crumbled the soil away with his fingers and stared at the lead soldier in his hand. Huge, hot tears which he could not control oozed out of his eyes and he sobbed. His mother comforted him and when he felt better he wanted to tell her everything.

"Wait a moment while I get Dad," she said gently. "He will want to know too." In a few minutes she was back with Dad and Rob, who seemed to have lost some of his usual bounce. Sam noticed, too, that the inspector had come in and was sitting on a hard chair at the back of the room out of the way.

With his parents close beside him, Sam explained how he had first seen the boy and mentioned it to them, thinking he was a neighbour. He explained how he saw the boy often and that he knew he was a child from another time. As he described how happy and content he had been in the ghost boy's company, Sam's parents realised how they had neglected him and how lonely he must have been. "He never spoke. I don't know who he was, but I think he lived here," Sam concluded.

"It's very strange," commented Dad. "Is there any way we can check about people missing a hundred years ago?"

The police inspector spoke for the first time. "I'm not sure how far back our records go. Leave it with me. We have to identify the body."

"I know the Press will want to report the skeleton. Is there any need to let them know what Sam has told us?" asked Dad. "I would prefer it if we could keep that to ourselves for the moment. The boy has had a strange experience."

"No need to mention it to them at all, sir. You can rely on me."

"Thank you," said Dad gratefully, and he showed the officer out.

Chapter VIII

The days that followed were quiet. The police had finished with the garden. Dad completed the drains and started to build up the wall again. When Sam felt fully recovered from his fall, his mother arranged for his friend, James, to come and spend a few days of half-term with them. The evening before James' visit, there was a knock at the door.

It was the police inspector. Mum invited him in. "I thought you would like to know what we've found out," he said. "I think you will find it interesting."

"Sit down," suggested Dad.

The inspector carried a folder. "There are some documents you might like to see," he said, spreading some papers on the table. "Here is a list of all the people who have lived in this house. As you see, it was built for a family called Armstrong and owned by them for nearly sixty years. After that, there were several others before you.

The people in the forensic department say that the body was over a hundred years old. It was a male child, about one metre forty centimetres in height. There was damage to the right side of the skull by the way." He glanced at Sam before he went on. "From the date of the bones, the body must have been buried while the house was owned by William Armstrong. From census records in 1871, we know he had a family of three daughters and two sons, John aged ten and Matthew aged four.

When we looked at the records for 1881, there was no mention of Matthew. He would have been fourteen by then. It was possible he could have been sent away to work, but we decided to do some more checking. A friend of mine in the archives has been sorting out the old newspapers. He came across this copy of the *Herald*, dated 1879." The police inspector pushed a photocopy of an old newspaper towards Sam's father.

NO NEWS OF MISSING BOY

There is still no news of Matthew Armstrong, aged twelve of Moss Bank, near Bampton, missing from home since Oct 15. He went to spend the day with a neighbour, Mrs Wilson, while his parents attended to business in town. Soon after he arrived, he told Mrs Wilson he had forgotten to feed the hens. He set off home, saying he would be back directly. Mrs Wilson was not immediately concerned when he was late for lunch as she said boys often wander off. When she finally sent her son looking for him without success, she became worried. By evening a search of the whole village was conducted, but this revealed no trace of the child.

Mr Joseph Chilman, a travelling worker, who was employed at the time by Mr Amstrong building walls, said he had worked all day and he had seen no one. It appears that the child did not reach home because the hens were still locked up. Enquiries are being made further afield.

The inspector paused before he showed them another paper. "I followed it up in the next newspaper, but you see there are only a few lines."

HOPES FADE FOR ARMSTRONG BOY

There is still no news of Matthew Armstrong, missing from his home at Moss Bank. It was later discovered that a gold watch, belonging to Mr Armstrong, is also missing. It is not known if the two events are connected.

"Oh! That makes it sound as if Matthew stole the watch and ran away," said Mum indignantly.

"Perhaps that's the only explanation they could think of," replied the inspector.

"I wonder why they didn't suspect Joseph Chilman," asked Dad.

"Those travelling workmen would be hard to track down," replied the inspector. "Anyway I shall hand all this over to the coroner at the inquest, and he will decide."

"Sam won't have to give evidence, will he?" asked Mum alarmed.

"I see no reason to call Sam. Nothing he could say could really be called evidence, whatever *we* think about it privately," he answered.

In the following weeks the mystery story of a hundred years ago was re-opened in the Press. The coroner accepted the evidence, in which it seemed likely that the body was that of Matthew Armstrong. He declared an open verdict on the boy's death, which meant no one could be sure how he died or who had buried him. Matthew Armstrong could now be properly buried.

The reporters wrote that the finger of suspicion must point to Joseph Chilman. As Sam read the reports with his mother, he felt sorry for Chilman. "He didn't kill him, I know that. I expect he thought no one would believe him," he said.

"He was probably right about that," said Mum. "So he just got away as fast as he could. He was lucky not to be found, though he would have to carry that secret all his life."

"Poor man. Poor Matthew," said Sam. "I'm glad we found him," he added. "Even if I don't see him again, I still have this as a reminder." And Sam turned over his most treasured possession in his hand, the small lead soldier.